In the same **Pomelo the Garden Elephant** series :

Pomelo Begins to Grow

First American edition published in 2012 by
Enchanted Lion Books, 20 Jay Street, Studio M-18, Brooklyn, NY 11201
Translation copyright © 2012 by Enchanted Lion Books
Translated by Claudia Zoe Bedrick
Originally published in France by Albin Michel Jeunesse © 2011 as **Pomelo et les couleurs**
All rights reserved under International and Pan-American Copyright Conventions
A CIP record is on file with the Library of Congress
ISBN: 978-1-59270-126-1
Printed in June 2012 in China by Toppan Leefung

Pomelo

Ramona Bădescu   Benjamin Chaud

Explores Color

ENCHANTED LION BOOKS
NEW YORK

When everything begins
to seem black and white,
Pomelo looks around and
suddenly rediscovers…

**the silent white
of the blank page**

the infinite white
of winter

the foamy white
of hot milk

**the comforting white
of his favorite dandelion**

the white of the eye

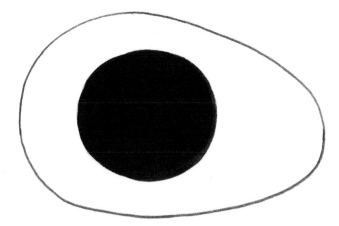

and the white of an egg

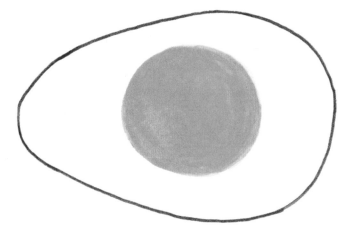

(which are almost the same)

**the always different
yellow of wee-wee**

the banana yellow
of some garden potatoes

the blinding yellow
of noon

the acidic yellow
of lemon

the glowing yellow
of fireflies

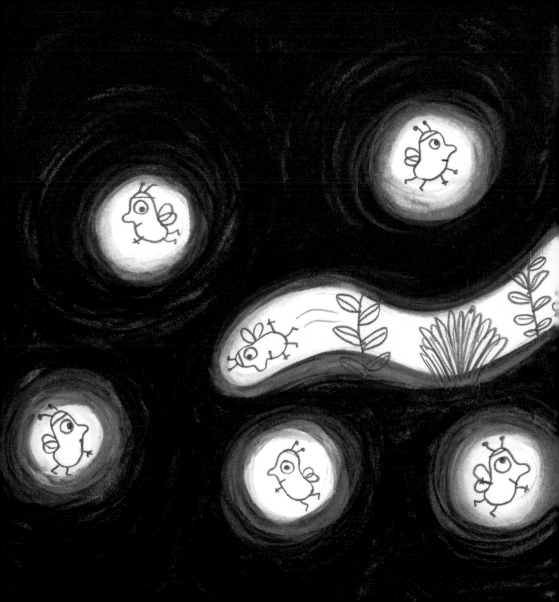

**the mustard-yellow pang
that goes up the nose**

canary yellow

(cheep-cheep)

the tender yellow
of young dandelions

the fiery orange
of sunset

the melancholy orange
of autumn

**the speeding orange
of shredded carrots**

the experimental orange
of experimental grass

the true orange
of an orange

the promising red
of ripening strawberries

the hypnotizing red
of love

**the surprising red
of ripe tomatoes**

**the explosive red
of anger**

the starry-eyed pink
of romance

the perfect pink
of Pomelo

the protective pink
of pink lettuce

the messy brown
of muddy earth

the shiny brown
of chestnuts

the breathtaking brown of Gigi

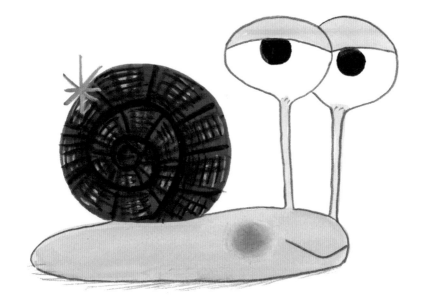

the puzzling purple
of eggplant

the hushed purple
of lavender

the revealing purple
of juicy blueberries

the energizing purple
of turnips

the lilac purple
of Pomelo

(if he were a granny)

the invisible violet
of ultraviolet

the mysterious blue
of dreams

the swirling blue
of the sky

the icy blue of winter

the dark blue-black
of night

the shadowy blue
of the Unknown

the blue-green
of water

**the perfect green
of garden peas**

the super-tremendous-heart-thumping green of Rita

the dismal green
of doubt

the joyful new green
of spring

the velvety green
of summer leaves

the bouncy green
of the meadow

the unchanging green
of fir trees

**the muddy green
that comes after the rain**

the green-gray
of rot

the deflating gray
of disappointment

the fantastic gray
of elephants

the silver gray
of pencil sketches

the gray of things
you can't quite remember

the dangerous gray
of stones

**the happy gray
of rain**

**the beguiling black
of mystery**

**the dashing black
of adventure**

**the magnificent black
fade-out of endings**

Now that Pomelo has had a chance to explore, he's TICKLED PINK to be one of the colors of our beautiful multicolored world.

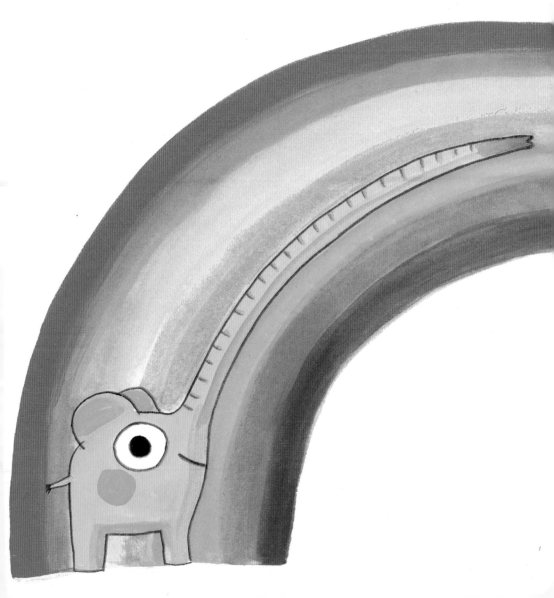